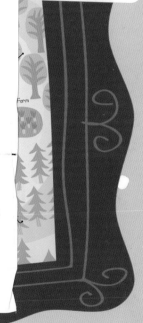

Adventure

...adventure starts at the Little Castle . . .

It's Christmas Eve and Father Christmas has come to the Little Kingdom.
"I'm in disguise!" he whispers to Ben and Holly. "I've come to see how the Christmas preparations are going!"

"Well, the elves have finished making all the toys," says the Wise Old Elf. "Mr Elf has been delivering them to the North Pole."

"Very good," says Father Christmas. "What about the Christmas crackers?"

The fairies are in charge
of the Christmas crackers
and Nanny Plum is in
charge of the bangs.
The bangs are very loud.

BANG!
BANG!

"We do the cracker-making underground because it's so noisy," explains Queen Thistle.

"The fairies use magic to put the crackers together," says the Wise Old Elf. "Then Mr Elf delivers the crackers to the shops. The Big People have no idea the crackers are made by elves and fairies!"

"Jolly good work," says Father Christmas. "What about the Christmas trees?"

5

"The pine elves, who live in the Great Pine Tree, have been growing the trees all year," the Wise Old Elf tells Father Christmas. "The Big People cut them down and have no idea they are grown by us Little People."

PARP!
PARP!

"Well, everything seems to be in hand," says Father Christmas.
"Thank you, elves and fairies! I'd better go back to the North Pole
and get ready to deliver the Christmas presents! Goodbye!"

7

THUMP!

THUMP!

THUMP!

What's that thumping noise?
The Wise Old Elf climbs the Great Pine Tree
to find out. "It's the Big People!" he cries.
The Big People have cut down the Great
Pine Tree! They take it away with the
pine elves and the Wise Old Elf inside.

CRASH!

SNAP!

TIMBER

LOG 1

8

HUMP!

THUMP!

THUMP!

SHRINK!

SHRINK!

SHRINK!

Back at the Little Castle, Queen Thistle
and Nanny Plum hear giant footsteps.
"The Big People are coming!" cries Nanny Plum. She
shrinks the Little Castle so the Big People won't see it.
"Help!" says the queen. "You've shrunk me, too!"

The giant footsteps belong to Father Christmas. "A toy castle!" he says. "I didn't know the elves were making these."
He takes the Little Castle – and the little Queen Thistle – back to the North Pole to be wrapped up as a Christmas present.

HELP! HELP!

King Thistle is very confused when he realizes the Little Castle is gone. He tries to call Father Christmas for help. Suddenly he gets magicked inside a Christmas cracker! Then the crackers are loaded on to the Elf Plane!

Oh dear! The Christmas preparations are no longer going very well. The Wise Old Elf is stuck inside a Christmas tree . . .

12

. . . Queen Thistle is wrapped up in a Christmas present . . .

. . . and King Thistle is trapped inside a Christmas cracker.

What a mess!

Ben and Holly's friend Lucy is shopping with her mum and dad.
"I'm looking forward to a quiet family Christmas this year, with no talk
of fairies and elves," says Lucy's dad. "Now which tree shall we get?"

"That one!" says Lucy, pointing to the Great Pine Tree.
"Yes, and let's get this box of crackers," says Lucy's mum.

At the Top-secret Elf Command Tracking Centre in the Little Kingdom, the elves are following Father Christmas's journey as he delivers presents to the children of the world.

"The flashing red dot on the screen shows where Father Christmas is," explains Mr Elf.
"Look!" says Holly. "He's nearly at Lucy's house!"

Father Christmas delivers his last parcel —
a present for Lucy. He is very tired.
"That chair looks comfy," he says with a big
yawn. "I'll just have a little sit-down . . ."
He closes his eyes and is soon fast asleep.

"Oh no! Look at Father Christmas!" cries Nanny Plum.
"We'll have to wake him up before he's discovered," says Mr Elf.
"Everyone! To the Elf Helicopter!"

19

"How lovely to have a nice, normal family Christmas without any weird magical stuff!" says Lucy's dad on Christmas morning.

Then King Thistle drops out of a cracker . . .

Bang!

. . . Lucy unwraps the Little Castle and the little Queen Thistle . .

Vroom!

. . . the Elf Helicopter
arrives . . .

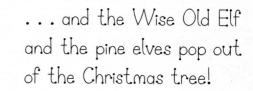

. . . and the Wise Old Elf
and the pine elves pop out
of the Christmas tree!

"Elves and fairies," groans Lucy's dad.
"All we need now is Father Christmas!"

"**Ho! Ho! Ho!**
Merry Christmas, everyone!"

"I give up," says Lucy's dad. "There's nothing else for it — you'll all have to join us for Christmas lunch!"

22

So they do – along with some more magical friends.

Merry Christmas, Ben and Holly!
Merry Christmas, Lucy!
Merry Christmas, everyone!

See you soon!